DEFENDERS

DARK ARENA

DEFENDERS
DARK ARENA

TOM PALMER

With illustrations by
David Shephard

For Amy and Hannah Manser,
a story about your city

First published in 2017 in Great Britain by
Barrington Stoke Ltd
18 Walker Street, Edinburgh, EH3 7LP

www.barringtonstoke.co.uk

Text © 2017 Tom Palmer
Illustrations © 2017 David Shephard

The moral right of Tom Palmer and David Shephard
to be identified as the author and illustrator of this work has
been asserted in accordance with the Copyright, Designs and
Patents Act, 1988

A CIP catalogue record for this book is available
from the British Library upon request

ISBN: 978-1-78112-730-8

Printed and bound by CPI Group (UK) Ltd, Croydon, CR0 4YY

They took in the scene below. A dense, dusty crowd of slaves poured from the amphitheatre. Among them were Roman soldiers in red cloaks and silver helmets, thrashing at the broken men with whips.

Seth turned from the dark arena. "We have to get away from here," he said. "Now."

1

A hundred and twenty-five metres above the earth, the crane cab began to rock. Olga had a sudden lurch of unease. The day was clear and calm, and so she gazed across London to check everything was how it should be.

The River Thames was a silvery thread, widening as it flowed out to sea.

A carpet of buildings and parks and roads spread out in all directions.

A queue of aircraft heading towards Heathrow was a line of fairy lights connecting the capital of the UK to the rest of the world.

Everything was normal. Beautiful, even. And then Olga looked down.

That was when she saw them.

There were dozens.

A slow-moving mass of bodies, intent on their purpose. Their hair was long, their feet bare. Ragged clothes hung from their filthy bodies like sacks. Their faces were blackened with dirt, their skulls pressed against thin skin. Some had bloody gashes on their arms and legs. Each one was holding a heavy wooden weapon as they climbed steadily upwards.

They looked like a cast of zombies from the TV series that Olga and her husband were addicted to. Actors playing the part of the walking dead. But these were no actors. In the window of her cab, Olga caught a reflection of her own eyes staring back at her, wild with fear.

What was this?

Who were they?

What did they want?

And now she could hear them. They were chanting some terrible rhythm of unknown words over and over again as they moved towards her.

Olga felt the strength drain from her. She put a hand to her mouth, feeling the burn of vomit in her throat. With her left hand, she leaned to press the emergency button, but she knew she had no chance of rescue before the mass of bodies reached her.

*

Minutes later, at the foot of the crane – the tallest

in England – a shocked huddle of workers in orange hard hats stood around the body of Olga Holub. The fall had smashed her flesh and bone and muscle into pieces – but her face was undamaged.

Her amber eyes stared up at the sky in terror, as if she had seen something beyond understanding before she fell.

2

"This is your room, Mrs White," the nurse said, holding the door open.

Seth hesitated and peered into the small room at the far end of Ward 5. It was warm and felt safe, so Seth followed the two adults inside.

Seth and his mum had come on the train from Halifax to London that day with Seth's friend Nadiya and his dog, Rosa. But this was no holiday in the capital. Seth's mum was seriously ill. She needed a week's specialist treatment, which, if it went to plan, would help her get well again.

That's why they were here. Seth tried not to think about what would happen if the treatment failed. Seth only had his mum. His dad was dead and he didn't have a brother or sister. There was no one else.

The nurse was still talking to Seth's mum in his calm and funny way, trying to make everyone relax. But Seth felt far from relaxed. He had a pain deep in his gut that throbbed through his body in waves. Seth didn't want to show he was hurting. He wanted his mum to think he was fine.

After all, she was the one who was ill.

"I'll leave you to settle in," the nurse said. "My name's Rafik. I'll be on the desk outside if you need me, and the doctor will be along soon."

Seth looked around. A bed. A TV. A bedside

table. A bunch of wires and tubes coming out of the wall at the head of the bed. A window with a white blind.

The room made Seth feel queasy. He hated hospitals. People died in places like this. Or, at least, were very ill – so ill that they might die.

Like his mum.

Seth stared out of the window. They were high up on the eleventh floor, meaning he could see across London. His gaze was drawn to a cluster of tower blocks to the east. Then – further north – to two incredibly tall cranes on a massive building site.

Seth turned from the window, uneasy.

There was another person in the room.

A woman with white hair and a lined face was looking at a vase of flowers, touching the petals and smiling.

Seth knew she wasn't real. Not any more.

The figure he could see was a ghost. She was a shadow of the person she had been before. Seth was used to these shadows. He saw them all the time and they didn't scare him. It was something he'd thought was normal until his mum said it wasn't, told him it used to happen to his dad too.

But Seth's dad had died before Seth was born. This ability to sense people from the past was something Seth shared with his dad. And for that reason he cherished it.

Sometimes Seth saw ghosts that weren't just shadows. These ghosts had unfinished business with the world. Other people could see them too – and they were the dangerous ones. But Seth knew this woman was just someone who had died in this room. She wasn't going to bother his mum.

"You'd better go back down now and see

Nadiya," his mum said. "Rosa will be getting restless."

Seth looked at his mum, struck by a sudden, sickening fear that she could be a shadow soon too.

3

Seth ran down the stairs to get out of the hospital – eleven floors, 25 stairs a floor. It felt good to burn off some of the tension from Ward 5. There were three lifts Seth could have used, but he didn't like lifts. He could never work out if you were supposed to speak to people. The silence unnerved him.

The stairs were a million times better.

His footsteps echoed as he ran.

A man in a dressing gown came up the other

way. His footsteps weren't making any sound at all. The man was a shadow too. This was a cancer hospital. Its rooms and corridors and stairwells were bound to be full of the shadows of people who'd died there.

But not Seth's mum.

She was going to live. She had to.

Outside Seth filled his lungs with air that felt brilliantly cool and fresh after the stale warmth of the hospital. Just then Rosa came springing across the lawn in front of the hospital doors. Her two front paws pushed hard against Seth, but he leaned into her lunge, so she didn't topple him over.

Seth grounded his dog on the grass and stroked her. He looked up to see Nadiya, his best friend from school. She was holding a ragged womble in one hand and Rosa's lead in the other.

"She broke the lead." Nadiya laughed. "I'm sorry."

"It breaks all the time," Seth said. "I need to buy a new one."

"How was it?" Nadiya asked, her voice cautious.

Seth stood up. "Fine. Nice for a hospital. Shall we go?"

"What shall I do with this?" Nadiya held out the stuffed womble.

Seth took it. "Sorry," he said. "It's kind of Rosa's comfort toy."

Nadiya led them all out of the car park to the tube station, heading for her aunt's house. Nadiya's family had offered to look after Seth for the week that his mum was in hospital. They'd even said he could bring Rosa too.

That's what Seth was thinking about as they walked to the tube station.

Rosa staying in someone else's house.

What could possibly go wrong?

A lot.

For starters, they had a cat. Rosa always chased cats. But Nadiya's aunt had said the cat would be fine. That it would all be OK.

Rosa and a cat? Seth didn't think for a minute that would turn out OK.

4

"How was your mother?" Nadiya's aunt asked Seth as she opened the door to them. "Has she settled in at the hospital?"

"Yes, thanks," Seth said, holding Rosa on the shortest possible lead.

They were standing in a narrow hall. Seth had already spotted a grey and white cat with a blue collar sitting at the top of the stairs. Its eyes like lasers on Rosa.

"That's Gus." Nadiya grinned.

Seth smiled back.

"And how do *you* feel?" the aunt asked.

"Fine, thanks," Seth replied automatically.

But Seth understood that he wasn't fine. He was tired and his head hurt. He wanted to be back at home in Halifax. If he was home now, he'd take Rosa for a long run out onto the moors and scream and shout into the wind. Or he'd curl up and lose himself in a pile of his dad's old superhero comics.

He felt Rosa's lead go tight as her nose pointed up the stairs. The cat glared down at Rosa and hissed, then turned and strolled into the shadows.

Seth knew that Nadiya's family were being very kind to let him stay. He had to be polite. He had to be a good guest. He couldn't run and hide like he wanted to.

And he already owed Nadiya a big favour.

Not long ago, back in Halifax, he'd seen some truly frightening shadows. Thanks to Nadiya he'd understood that they were shadows of a massacre – of Vikings and their Anglo-Saxon victims. And so Seth and Nadiya had ended the suffering of those who were slaughtered hundreds of years ago.

They'd worked well together. Made good defenders, as Nadiya put it. Defenders of those who had suffered terrible wrongs in the past.

Meanwhile, at the foot of the stairs, no one had spoken for a second or two. Seth could imagine what Nadiya's aunt was thinking. Here was a boy whose mum was really ill, who might die. A boy whose dad had died years ago. A boy who might soon be an orphan. Seth knew he should fill the silence before it grew impossible.

"The hospital is great," he said. "They'll do everything they can to make my mum better."

Another silence. Even longer this time. Nadiya kept opening her mouth as if she wanted to speak, but didn't know what to say.

Seth looked around. There was an old-fashioned portrait of a young couple near the door. The man, dark-haired and handsome in a suit, the woman in a sparkling sari.

"Who are they?" he asked.

"My grandparents," Mrs Alam said proudly, glad to have something to say. "They emigrated from India in 1947. My grandfather worked in the railways for a few years, then he started a printing business and they bought this house and commissioned this painting to celebrate. In the background is the ship they travelled on from India to England."

Seth smiled and nodded. He liked the story.

Mrs Alam led Seth and Nadiya into the front

room. Big white leather sofas took up two of the walls and a round mirror hung above the fireplace.

Mrs Alam brought in a tray of tea and a plate full of sticky orange sweets shaped almost like flowers.

"They're called jalebi," she told Seth. "Help yourself – they're delicious!"

As Seth devoured three of the sweets – he hadn't realised how hungry he was – Mrs Alam asked them, "So, what are your plans for tomorrow?"

"We're going on a history tour," Nadiya answered, her voice gleeful.

"Really?" Mrs Alam said, giving Seth a look of pity.

Seth laughed – Mrs Alam knew her niece well.

As soon as Nadiya had known they were going to stay with her aunt and uncle, she'd

been obsessed. She was desperate to take Seth to London's most famous historical sites and see if his gift of seeing shadows worked in the capital too. If he could see shadows of the past in Halifax, surely he'd be able to see ghosts in London. If he could, then she wanted him to tell her all about them – what they wore, what they were doing, what their faces looked like.

"Yes," Nadiya said. "Seth is really into history, like me. We can't wait."

It was certainly true that she couldn't wait. She'd already asked him if he thought he'd see kings and queens on London's streets. Or just ordinary people. Seth had told her he had no idea. Nadiya would have to wait and see.

5

That evening the Alam family settled down to watch TV. There was a lot of them – Nadiya's aunt, her uncle home from work, and her cousins, Dilip, Rahul and Sunil, who were on the floor, playing with Rosa. Rosa was lying on her back looking like she was in heaven. The cat was nowhere to be seen.

They were watching a cartoon about the adventures of a boy and his dog. The dog could shape-shift – a trick to save them from a constant stream of danger. Nadiya's uncle kept asking questions. *Why did the cartoon dog do this? Why did the boy want that?* Seth thought it was funny how desperate he was to change the channel.

Then Seth noticed that there were two more people in the room.

Shadows.

More shadows.

A woman wearing a spectacular pink and gold sari that glittered like it was made of tiny mirrors. A man in an immaculate dark suit. They were smiling and – like everyone else – looking at the TV screen.

As well as seeing them, Seth could smell something. A nice light smell, like fresh herbs, but sweet.

Seth remembered the portrait in the hall. The painting of Nadiya's great-grandparents new to the

UK, the ship behind them. The couple in the room had the same smiling faces, just older.

"It's them," Seth said.

"Sorry, Seth," Nadiya's aunt said. "It's who? Who is who?"

Seth felt himself go cold as he realised he'd spoken out loud.

Awkward.

Nadiya's three cousins were staring at Seth now, smiles on their faces, their eyes sparkling, expecting something funny to happen.

Nadiya was staring too, trying to work out what Seth was on about. Was it something on the TV? But she said nothing. She'd ask him later.

Seth coughed and tried to recover the situation. "Sorry. I must have been dreaming." He yawned. "It's been a long day."

He was cross with himself. It was one thing

seeing shadows of the past. It was another telling people about it.

Seeing that Seth was confused and embarrassed, Mrs Alam got to her feet. "Children. Upstairs now and get ready for bed. *Now*. Seth's had a stressful day. Go on."

The three boys stood up and hugged their mum and dad, then Nadiya. Then they approached Seth and each, in turn, put their hand out to shake his.

Seth wanted to smile, but he kept his face straight. It was nice, a welcoming gesture, and he didn't want them to think he was mocking them.

As soon as the boys were out of the room, Mr Alam changed channels.

"Shall we watch something more meaningful?" He grinned as the News came on.

Seth's eyes glazed over during a piece about infighting among MPs, but the next story made him

sit up straight. It was about a new football stadium being built in London. There had been an awful – and strange – accident.

A crane operator working on the site of London's new Morti Stadium has fallen over one hundred metres to her death. Accident investigators from the Health & Safety Executive have closed the site while they ascertain what caused the tragedy. Construction of the stadium is both complex and sensitive – it is being built over the site of a recently discovered Roman amphitheatre.

Seth remembered the cranes he'd seen from his mum's hospital window. He wondered if the dead woman had been in one of them.

The Italian-based stadium owners – the international sports company Renaissance – have expressed their sorrow and support for the family of the dead crane operator, Olga Holub.

"As if they'd care about anyone's family," Nadiya scoffed. "I hate Renaissance."

"No, Nadiya." Mr Alam tutted. "There's no need to hate any one."

"But I do, Uncle," Nadiya insisted, suddenly animated. "And I'll tell you why! They're the ones who make all those cheap sports clothes in sweatshops in Sri Lanka. The workers are like slaves – paid almost nothing and they're nearly all woman and children. And the factories are really unsafe – like, if there's even a small fire, workers die and are badly hurt. I've read about it. There's loads of evidence against them."

Seth smiled. Nadiya was fierce!

"OK, Nadiya," Mr Alam conceded. "Perhaps they are hateful, but that doesn't change things for that poor woman who died."

6

"You saw them, didn't you?"

Nadiya stared at Seth as she spoke. They had just left her aunt and uncle's house and were walking along rows of neat terraced houses, shaded by the trees that lined the road. Rosa ran ahead of them, her nose to the ground, taking in the new smells of the city on this mild, sunny morning.

"So, did you?" Nadiya didn't wait for an answer. "See my great-grandparents?"

"Yes."

"And?"

"And they were just standing there," Seth said. "They were wearing their best clothes and smiling. Like they were watching TV with your family."

"That's nice," Nadiya said, her stare softening. "I never met them. They died before I was born. I thought you'd see famous people from history here, not my ancestors. What did they look like?"

"Your great-grandmother was wearing a sari," Seth said. "It sparkled as if it was made of stars. And your great-grandfather had a fantastic suit on. They looked amazing. They were happy. I could tell."

"Did they look at me?" Nadiya's voice dropped. "Did they know who I am?"

"I don't know for sure," Seth replied. "But I'd guess so. They smiled when they looked over at you."

"Will you tell me," Nadiya said, taking Seth's arm, "if you see them tonight? And show me where they are?"

"Yes," Seth said. "But let's go and see what other London ghosts we can find, shall we?"

7

They took the underground into the city. Seth had no idea where they were going and was just tagging along with Nadiya, enjoying the sensation of being in London.

But Rosa was stressed by the rattle and thunder of the train along the dark tunnels, leaning into Seth, growling quietly if she saw someone she didn't like the look of.

Then they were out of the train and up some

steps. Rosa was pulling hard on her lead now.

Then, standing in a long queue on an escalator, Seth picked Rosa up to make sure she didn't get caught in the moving stairs. They were in the midst of hundreds of people, wearing colourful scarves and coats and chatting in different languages.

"Tourists," Nadiya said with a grin. "Just like us!"

Seth followed Nadiya into the bright sunshine outside Tower Hill tube station. He spotted a huge castle opposite with the River Thames behind it.

"Where are we?" he asked.

"It's the Tower of London." Nadiya laughed. "Don't you know anything?"

Seth smiled. "I don't get out much."

But he knew exactly why they were at the Tower of London. It was a place of serious history. A place where Nadiya would want him to tell her what he could see. Seth gazed around. In among the modern city buildings, the stalls packed with every kind of souvenir and the mad bustle of tourists, he could see people dressed in long white garments. Some had thick woollen capes over their shoulders. Then there were the working men and women whose clothes appeared to be made of rough sackcloth.

Shadows. Shadows from the past.

Then a pair of figures he did recognise.

"I can see two centurions," he told Nadiya. "Roman soldiers. In plumed helmets with guards at the side for their ears and faces. They've got bright silver chest plates on. And long red capes with buckles."

"Really?" Nadiya's eyes shone. "What's happening?"

"Nothing much. They're just stood there."

"What about Caesar – is he there? And can you see any headless queens or princes?"

"Er ... no," Seth said.

"But we're at the Tower of London."

"So, do you want to go in?" Seth asked.

"I'm not sure now." Nadiya sounded disappointed.

"OK," he said. "Maybe tomorrow."

Nadiya led Seth away from the Tower. Across busy roads with buses, taxis and lorry engines roaring.

"Where now?" Seth asked, a taste in his mouth like metal from the exhaust fumes.

"Anywhere," Nadiya said. "I'm just curious to know what you see."

And so they walked the streets, going deeper into the city of London. Some of the buildings were made of stone so solid they looked like they'd never

fall down. Others were towering structures of shiny black glass, reflecting the clouds. The height and closeness of the buildings crowded Seth. He missed the wide open sky. It felt like there was a lot more sky at home.

"There's a man coming towards us in a long white cape," Seth said. "He's got a crown of green leaves on ..."

"Who is he?"

"I don't know. And now there's a carriage with a woman sitting at the front. She's got a whip and she's forcing the horses on."

Seth covered his ears against the rattle of carriage wheels on the ground. Nadiya stared at him, then down at the road.

Seth came to a sudden stop. Deep in the pit of his stomach he felt a clutch of fear, a dreadful darkness.

"What is it?" Nadiya asked. "What's the matter?"

Seth didn't reply. Up until now all the shadows had been like a historical film projected onto a cinema screen. But now there was something else up ahead. Something that wasn't like a shadowy film at all.

Seth shivered.

"Seth?"

He felt Nadiya's hand on his arm.

"What's that way?" Seth asked, pointing up at a high metal fence, a pair of tall cranes towering over the buildings all around.

Nadiya's gaze followed Seth's, but she already knew the answer to his question.

"That's where they're building the stadium that was on the news last night," she said. "Where they're preserving the Roman amphitheatre. The place where that woman died."

8

The first thing Seth noticed about the building site was the sky.

Above the Morti Stadium there was a vast space and that space was full of light. With no buildings cluttering the skyline, Seth's gaze could roam among the clouds. It was a relief from the penned-in feeling he'd had a few moments ago.

"You OK?" Nadiya asked. "You looked a bit spooked back there."

"Yeah, I was." Seth nodded. "But it's OK. I want to see what it is, why I felt like that."

They walked towards a fence made of blue metal sheets bolted together. It was like every other building site – dangerous and full of expensive equipment and materials. This perimeter fence was designed to keep people out and building stuff in.

But this fence also had gaps where you could view what was going on inside. A sign above each gap read.

FIND OUT ABOUT LONDON'S AMPHITHEATRE HERE

This amphitheatre was built between the years AD 50 and AD 100. At first it was a timber structure around an arena dug into the natural sands. Wooden bench seating was erected for the audience to watch wild animal fights and gladiatorial action.

From AD 150 external stone walls were built and the entrance way was made of stone too. The majority of the workers who built the amphitheatre were slaves belonging to their Roman masters.

Seth and Nadiya joined a queue to view the amphitheatre. As they waited, Seth noticed five or six security guards, all wearing high-vis jackets with the word MORTI printed on the back.

But there were other guards too. These men wore suits and had earpieces in. Seth squinted and noticed they all had their bulky jackets done up, even though the day was scorching.

"What are they hiding?" Seth asked himself. Surely they weren't armed? Why would a building site have so much security?

At last Seth and Nadiya reached the front of the queue.

When they looked through the wooden slot into the amphitheatre they saw layers of stone steps descending in a bowl-like shape, a flat arena at the centre. Above the excavated amphitheatre was the huge concrete and steel base of the new stadium.

"What can you see, Seth?" Nadiya asked. "Are there any gladiators? Animals? The Romans would have brought wild creatures here. Lions. Elephants. Bears. To fight each other. Can you see them?"

"No," Seth said, frowning.

"What then?"

"Hundreds of men in dirty rags," Seth said. "They're hauling and breaking stones. They look shattered. Some have collapsed."

His voice was low and tired and Seth felt dizzy with exhaustion, as if what he could see was draining him of all his energy. He stumbled and held himself up against the fence. He felt he might faint

and knew he'd gone pale from the look of concern of Nadiya's face. There was something about this place that was wrong. Really wrong. He felt sick with dread and fear. But he wanted to tell Nadiya more. Maybe if he kept talking, his feelings would start to make sense.

"There are more men in red cloaks and silver helmets," Seth went on. "Centurions. They've got whips and … and … they're striking out at … It's …"

"Are you OK?" Nadiya put her arm out to steady her friend.

Rosa was looking at Seth too, her eyes big and brown. Her instincts always told her when something was wrong.

"No," Seth said, turning from the desperate, dark scene in the arena before him. "We have to get away from here. Now."

9

"What was it?" Nadiya panted as they got away from the site. "What did you see that was so bad, Seth?"

They'd been walking fast for more than ten minutes before Seth would stop. Walking, but not talking.

At last, he came to a halt and stared over Nadiya's shoulder at the road they'd come down.

"There were hundreds," he said.

"Of what?"

"Didn't you see them?" Seth grabbed Nadiya's hand, not answering her.

"See who? No. I saw no one."

"Men – masses of men," Seth told her, his voice shaky. "It felt really really bad. And there was this horrible airless, dusty smell."

Nadiya knew she had to be careful. She said nothing, hoping Seth would elaborate. She could tell he was confused. What had he seen that had made him so upset?

"Men in rags," Seth said, after a pause. "Their hair long and tangled. Their bodies all scarred and grimy. Their feet bare."

"What were they wearing?"

"Rags. I told you," Seth snapped. "Just rough, torn material."

They were sitting on a bench opposite a huge

building made of white stone, ornate with columns and statues and steps. Nadiya recognised it as the Bank of England – one of the most important buildings in London, possibly the world.

"Were they carrying anything?" Nadiya pressed, curiosity getting the better of her.

"Tools," Seth replied. "Hammers. Chisels for working the stone."

Nadiya gasped. "Slaves," she said. "They must be slaves."

"What?"

"They were slaves. The people the Romans enslaved to help them build London. Britons. It said on the sign at the amphitheatre. You've seen slaves from two thousand years ago, Seth."

Seth shook his head. He couldn't quite grasp it, but he was pretty sure Nadiya was right.

Nadiya went on, "That bad feeling you get. Like

in Halifax, at the Shay – when you saw the Viking massacre of the villagers."

Seth didn't reply and Nadiya knew to hold back now. Even though she had a hundred more questions.

Seth nodded. "I'm not sure I could face that again," he said in a quiet voice, as he looked at his watch.

"It's nearly visiting time," Nadiya said.

Seth nodded again. The hospital. He was dreading it. How mad was that? He was dreading seeing his mum.

10

Head down, Seth walked along the corridor of Ward 5 on his own. The hospital air smelled funny. The bright white lights made his eyes ache. He didn't want to see any of the other patients, or notice any shadows. He just wanted to get to his mum's room.

Seth breathed in and out. Deep breaths to calm and prepare himself.

Then, footsteps and a kind voice behind him.

"Hello, Seth. Here to see your mum?"

Seth turned to see the nurse from the day before. Rafik.

"Yes," he said. "Please."

"You know she's begun her treatment," Rafik said, a note of caution sounding in his voice.

"I know," Seth said. "How will she be?"

"Asleep probably. But she'll know you're here, Seth. You can help her recover by talking to her."

"But what do I talk about?" Seth's nerves jangled like crazy. How was it he didn't know what to talk to his mum about?

They were outside her door now.

Rafik grinned. "You know how she usually asks you about your day at school and you don't really tell her anything, you just say it was fine?"

"Yeah." Seth smiled – how did this nurse know that?

"Well, today tell her the things she'd like to hear. The things that will make her proud. But only for half an hour. OK? You don't want to tire her out."

11

Seth was holding his mum's hand. She was unconscious. Or asleep. Seth wasn't quite sure what the difference was. When he started talking he thought he'd felt her squeeze his hand, but now he couldn't be sure. And so he went on.

"And after the Tower of London we walked up to where they're building the new stadium," Seth told her. "It was boiling hot and ..."

The lady with the flowers wasn't there. The

lights were dimmed low. He could hear knocking sounds coming from the next room as he talked.

"Then we looked in from this viewing area and saw where they're excavating the old amphitheatre. You'd have loved it. It's amazing. It was built of wood first, then stone. And the stone is still there – they're preserving it. You can actually see it, Mum. Nadiya told me all about what the amphitheatre would have been used for. Two thousand years ago ..."

Seth carried on talking. But it wasn't easy. He was struggling with waves of questions washing over him. And one question wouldn't go away. It hammered at his brain like the slaves pounding the rocks.

What if the treatment didn't work? What if Mum never woke up, never opened her eyes again? What if she was already dying?

Seth couldn't talk any more. He was trying to work out what he was feeling.

Dread.

That was the word for it. Dread. That overwhelming sense that something really bad was about to happen. And that he had no choice but to sit there and wait for it to happen.

Or not. Either way, he knew he couldn't feel like this all week.

"I hate this, Mum," Seth said, then wished he hadn't. He caught his breath. "So when you're better I'll take you there. Yeah? When you are better I'll show you the amphitheatre."

Seth needed something to distract him. He wanted to cry. Only to his mum. Not to anyone else. But he couldn't cry to his mum because he needed to be strong for her.

Seth had never felt so bad. He'd never wanted

his mum so much. But she couldn't comfort him now.

"There were security guards everywhere," Seth said, starting again. "Ones in high-vis jackets, but ones in suits too. I think they were armed. Like something out of a Bond film."

Seth talked and talked. He didn't tell his mum about the ghost slaves. He'd tell her when she was better. When at last he ran out of words, he listened to his mum breathing in and out. He smiled as he realised that her breathing was easy and regular.

As Seth sat there, something important came to him in a flash. There was only one way to stop feeling terrified by how ill his mum was. It was crazy, but he needed to be terrified by something else. But what?

Seth thought of Nadiya, outside with Rosa. He'd go down to see her and they would head over to the amphitheatre and face the horror waiting there. However dark and scary it was at the amphitheatre, it couldn't be as dark and scary as sitting in this room alone with his mum, hearing only her breath in response to his words.

12

Seth felt like there'd been a zombie apocalypse in London. It was as if everyone was dead and the city had been left to the wind and the gloom and the silent scuttling rats. The streets around the Morti Stadium were empty of people. A solitary car zoomed past every now and then.

Even Rosa was disinterested. No smells to smell. Nothing to chase.

Dead.

But Seth could see Roman sentries posted every hundred metres or so. They looked like the ones he'd seen near the Tower of London. Plumed metal helmets and shiny armour. Red capes. Leather boots strapped up to their knees.

But no one that wasn't a shadow. Where was everyone else? Where were the security guards he'd seen earlier?

The three of them reached the tall, sheer fence that surrounded the building site. Still no one. Only the muffled sound of low, urgent voices. And scuffling.

There was a door marked 'restricted entry' in the fence, but it was ajar, clearly unlocked.

Excited, Nadiya tugged Seth's arm. But Seth held back, hesitant, and Rosa whimpered too, pressing herself against his leg. Why was the building site open? Why was it unguarded? Nothing seemed right.

"Shall we?" Nadiya asked, her eyes shining in the dark.

"I suppose so," Seth replied. "I feel so strange and I need to find out what that means."

It was true. Seth needed to know.

"Come on then," he said, dragging Rosa along on her lead. "We're going in."

13

The three of them crept through the unlocked door and then onto rough wooden planks laid together to form a walkway. They came out into an open area with the old amphitheatre below, and the concrete and steel shell of the new stadium above. Around the amphitheatre were banners, showing a stark image of a Roman eagle with its huge wings outstretched.

Rosa wagged her tail. She'd lost her nerves and now wanted to explore.

Seth let her off the lead. He knew she'd come back if he called her.

Powerful floodlights, brighter than daylight, lit the amphitheatre excavation pit. Seth realised that this meant the shadows were extra dark. They could look around at the site away from the edges of the pit and not be spotted by security guards watching on CCTV.

Seth led the way towards a steep staircase. The blocks of stone that made the steps were massive, as if built for giants. Each stone was labelled with a black number on a square of white plastic.

The further down the steps they went, the more Seth felt overcome by that odd, bleak feeling. His head throbbed. And something kept catching in his throat. He felt unnerved, but the sense of despair wasn't strong enough to force him to turn back.

"Maybe this will be OK," he told himself. Maybe he'd find the source of his bad feelings and that would make them go away.

Nadiya kneeled down and placed her palms flat on the steps, absorbing the cold of the stone. Seth knew she was thinking of the thousands of people who would have come here to watch the fighting. Men first. Then animals. Spectators would have relished the killing. The bloody brutality of it. Nadiya couldn't imagine how anyone could watch men and animals tear one another apart in a fight to the death.

"Can you see animals?" she asked, wanting to understand.

"No," Seth said and he held up his hand to silence his friend. Again he could hear something muffled. Shuffling. Mumbling.

What *was* it?

They climbed down, keeping to the shadows, aware of the presence of cameras and guards – somewhere.

At the bottom there was another set of doors in another fence. Just like the ones they'd come through at the top. This was where the muffled sounds were coming from.

Now they had a choice. Should they walk around the bottom of the amphitheatre or open the doors?

"Can you hear that noise?" Seth asked Nadiya. "From behind the doors?"

"Like a machine?" Nadiya said. "Thumping?"

Seth nodded, nervous now. His heart tightened like it was held in an iron grip. He knew that the sensible thing to do would be to walk away.

"I'm going to open the doors," Seth said. "Stand back. Go up the steps."

"Why?" Nadiya asked.

"It could be dangerous."

"Come off it, Seth," Nadiya snapped. "I want to see it as much as you. Whatever it is."

Seth shrugged. He'd learned by now not to argue with her.

"Rosa," he called. "Here."

The dog ran over to be close to Seth. She'd sensed too that something was about to happen.

Seth pressed his hands against the door.

"Ready?" he asked.

"Ready." Nadiya grinned.

Seth took hold of the door's rough rope handles and pulled.

The doors were heavy and stiff. They didn't budge. He pulled again, putting all his strength into it this time.

14

Seth fell backwards as the doors swung open. Then
he felt them on top of him. A moving swarming
mass. Dozens and dozens of people. Stinking filthy
people.

Rosa ran, turning and barking again and
again. Nadiya watched in horror as men in rags,
thick with dust, landed on Seth, smothering him.
She screamed, then grabbed her friend and tugged
him backwards, out of the hands of two grasping

clutching figures who were pulling at his hair, his clothes, his face.

They scrambled to their feet.

"You can see them?" Seth shouted in panic, staring first at Nadiya, then back to the men.

Nadiya nodded. "Rosa can too. Look."

The dog was moving away from the men, growling, low to the ground, the fur on her back jagged like the teeth of a saw.

Then they ran full pelt.

Seth knew these were no harmless shadows of the past. If Nadiya and Rosa could see them, then they were real and the three of them were in grave danger.

"Up the steps," Nadiya gasped. "To the other door."

Seth followed, his mind a swirling mess, no space for ordered thoughts. He had no idea how to

escape, so if Nadiya said up the steps, then he was going up the steps.

He lengthened his stride to take them at speed. Nadiya was two or three paces ahead of him. His lungs were burning, but, after his first burst of pure effort, he glanced back. The ragged men were far behind them. They were awkward, struggling to climb, taking much longer than Seth and Nadiya on each step.

But Seth could feel their intent, their deadly eyes fixed on the two of them.

"They're way off the pace!" Seth called up to Nadiya. "Look!"

Catching their breath, they paused to take in the scene below. A dense, shifting crowd of these people – or whatever they were – was pouring from the gap in the door at the base of the amphitheatre. And, among them, were those Roman soldiers again, thrashing at the dusty, broken men with whips.

"Let's go," Seth said, unable to bear any more. "I need to get away from these … zombies."

"They are not zombies," Nadiya shouted.

"What are they then?"

"They're slaves," Nadiya said. "And the Roman soldiers are forcing them to work."

Seth stared at his friend. "Slaves?" he asked. "Ghosts of the slaves who built the amphitheatre?" At last he got it. He understood. "But why? Why now? The excavation has been going on for two years."

"I don't know," Nadiya replied. "But it's not good I can see them, is it?"

"No." Seth shivered as the iron-like grip on his heart tightened.

"Let's go," Nadiya said, watching him. "We can talk about what it all means when we're safe."

They turned and climbed the rest of the amphitheatre steps, Rosa jostling to be next to Seth. Out of the arena and back across the wooden boards to the door they'd first come through. Nadiya grabbed the handle and was about to pull it open when voices stopped her.

"Why isn't this locked?" A man, harsh and challenging.

"Sorry, sir. It should be." A woman.

"Then lock it," the gruff voice said. "Any lapses in security at the launch party tomorrow with the stadium owners and we're dead. Totally dead. Do you understand?"

"Yes, sir. Sorry, sir."

Seth and Nadiya listened to the clank-clang as the door was pulled tight, then locked.

In silence, they turned to see the mass of slave workers reach the top step of the amphitheatre.

Then the slaves started to move steadily across the wooden boards.

"We're trapped," Seth muttered as Rosa growled, low and menacing. "There's no way out. We're the ones who are dead."

15

Seth looked at Nadiya, then kneeled down and cupped his hands.

"Put your foot in my hands," he said, suddenly resolute. "I'll give you a leg up."

"What about you?"

"Forget me," Seth shouted. "Do it. You can try to unlock the other side. It's our only hope."

"No."

"Yes."

"NO!" Nadiya scowled at Seth.

"You know when I went into the Shay and confronted the Vikings?" Seth asked.

"Yeah," Nadiya said, still unconvinced.

"I did that because of something my mum said. She told me that before he died my dad said I should always do what I think is right. And I think it's right for me to get you over this door. So that's what I'm going to do. Move it."

Seth didn't like speaking like this to Nadiya. But it was the right thing to do. He glared at her, hoping she would agree.

At last Nadiya nodded, put her foot in Seth's hands and Seth lifted her up as she scrambled to the top of the fence.

With all his strength Seth heaved her over and heard her land on the other side.

Then he pushed Rosa into the small gap at the

foot of the fence. She wriggled through easily.

Seth turned around.

He was surprised they'd not reached him yet, not started to grab at him, pull at him, do whatever it is slave ghosts do to the living when they catch them. He remembered how a murderous Viking ghost had swung a heavy axe at him the last time he'd been in this sort of danger.

He had to face them, but ghosts could kill – if they wanted to.

The door behind him rattled as Nadiya struggled to open it. Rosa was barking madly. Seth pulled at the gate, but he knew it was hopeless.

16

When Seth turned he saw the slaves had stopped a few paces short of him. They were kneeling, their eyes reflecting the strong glare of the floodlights.

"*Angylesau*," one of them said.

And now they had their hands clasped, some leaning forward to touch their heads to the ground.

It was like the ghosts from before. When Seth had saved the Anglo-Saxons from a Viking massacre. Those families had stared at him in awe.

Angylesau. Seth knew that it meant angel. These men thought he was an angel.

But still, Seth's mind was scrambled. What should he do? He could hear Nadiya calling him, her voice anxious. Rosa's distressed barking. The rattle of the locks.

And then one of the slaves walked up to him, bent before him, then cupped his hands, like Seth had done for Nadiya.

Seth couldn't believe it. His heart was hammering so hard that waves of sickness were pulsing through his body. But now he could see the first of the Roman guards striding towards him, a long leather whip lashing its way through the slaves.

Screams.

Shouts.

The sound of flesh tearing under the snap of the whip.

Seth looked into the dark eyes of the slave whose hands were cupped to offer him a leg up.

"I'll be back," he told him.

The slave said something in reply. Something Seth could not understand. Then he put his foot in the slave's broad hands and felt strong arms lift him up.

He gripped the top of the fence and pushed himself over and down to the ground on the other side.

Rosa leaped up, nipping at him.

"How did you do that?" Nadiya stared at him.

"One of the slaves gave me a leg up."

"What!?"

"I'm serious. They helped me."

"OK ..." Nadiya said. "So, er ... what next?"

"We arm ourselves. Then we come back."

Nadiya stared at Seth, puzzled.

"Arm ourselves with knowledge." Seth smiled. "Not weapons."

"You mean history," Nadiya said. "Now you're talking."

17

Seth phoned the hospital first thing in the morning.

Nadiya and her aunt watched him. Rosa was sitting next to them, having her head scratched.

"What did the doctors say?" Nadiya's aunt asked when Seth finished the call.

"Mum's still unconscious," Seth told her. "It might be best for me to visit her tonight. Not this morning."

Nadiya's aunt stood up and put her arm round

Seth. "So much for a boy to deal with," she said, tears forming in her eyes.

"It's OK," he said quickly.

Nadiya's aunt shook her head. "No. It is not OK. But you are a credit to your mother and I will tell her that when I meet her one day."

Seth smiled and leaned into her arm. He liked that idea. It was good to hear about the future, not just worry about the present.

"So, do you have plans today?" she asked, turning to Nadiya.

"Yes, Aunt. The Museum of London. If ..." Nadiya looked down at Rosa.

"If I look after Rosa?" Her aunt grinned and hugged Nadiya as well. "I'd love to. By the time you get back she'll be best friends with Gus too."

18

A walk to the station, a train ride, then into the noisy chaos of buses and taxis and crowds pushing past Seth and Nadiya in the city streets.

They walked quickly. It seemed best to join in with the pace of London, rather than feel like you were forever in somebody's way. But it troubled Seth how relentless everything was, no time or space to look about or chat.

As they walked, Seth caught sight of an ornate,

yellow-white dome between two buildings. It was beautiful, majestic among the modern glass and metal towers.

"St Paul's Cathedral," Nadiya said, noticing. "Designed by Sir Christopher Wren after the fire of London."

They took a moment to gaze at it, then pressed on. Seth saw how well-dressed everyone seemed in this part of London. Everyone's shoes were polished and shiny, their suits crisp despite the heat. Seth suddenly felt scruffy in his trainers and jeans.

Up a set of steps they went and over a dual carriageway. They stopped to look at giant fragments of wall set among grassy lawns, where a group of children were having a picnic.

"That's London's old Roman wall," Nadiya said. "It's nearly two thousand years old."

Then the museum itself.

"There's a massive Roman section," Nadiya said, almost skipping with delight. "Come on, it's ace."

Seth's spirits lifted at the edge of excitement in Nadiya's voice, and he liked the museum too. The tiny models of Roman villas and bridges. The displays of tools and crockery recovered from cellars and river banks and tunnels. It was all arranged to reflect different aspects of life in Roman London.

It didn't take them long to find a display about slaves – there was a picture of men loading wooden crates onto a ship. Another with shabbily dressed people being herded onto boats in the docks. A vast banner above them showed a Roman eagle.

"See," Nadiya said. "The Romans took slaves back to Rome all the time."

"Britons?" Seth asked. "Like the ones we saw?"

Nadiya nodded.

And Seth understood that it was a connection that could help them solve the weird goings-on at the building site of the Morti Stadium.

19

In the museum café, Seth ordered a milkshake, Nadiya a glass of water with a slice of lemon. They bought a huge chocolate muffin to share.

Then they found a table in the far corner and sat down. Seth looked up from the museum notebook he'd just bought. The windows of the café looked out onto the streets of London and the Roman walls – and they were decorated with faded images of Londoners through the ages. Children begging. Men and women dressed in fine clothes.

Seth smiled. They looked a bit like the ghostly shadows he saw.

Nadiya fished the lemon out of her water with quick fingers, then ate it. Her face screwed up with the sharp taste.

"So, what do we know?" Nadiya asked.

"There are ghosts at the new stadium and amphitheatre," Seth said bluntly. "Loads of them. They look like slaves – Britons – that the Romans have forced to build their amphitheatre. And they're troubled."

"I agree," Nadiya said. "But why now? They've been building the stadium for two years – and there's been no trouble until this week. Nothing apart from that poor woman who fell from the crane."

Seth took a gulp of his milkshake, then a chunk of the muffin. The sugary combination tasted good.

But he had no answer to Nadiya's question.

"Last time," Nadiya said to fill Seth's silence. "Back home. The new floodlights triggered the haunting. They made that attack you witnessed echo through time. So, we need a link," she went on. "Something that has made the past haunt the present. Do you see? There has to be an awful thing happening now that's making the slaves appear."

"The sponsors," Seth gasped. "The stadium sponsors. The Italians. They use sweatshop labour to make their money. You said so. *That's* awful, really awful."

Nadiya pushed her chair back with a scraping noise.

"Slaves." She raised her voice. "You've got it, Seth. It's to do with slaves now and then. The ones from two thousand years ago need us to help the ones from today."

Seth knew straight away that she was right.

"And I think –" Nadiya grabbed her bag – "I know what we can do about it."

"What?"

"I've got a plan," Nadiya said. Then she smiled and told Seth what she thought they should do.

20

Ward 5 was busy when Seth got there that evening.

Visitors were arriving all at once, but there was something else going on too. An alarm rang out. Hospital staff were rushing to a room where a light flashed above the door. But it wasn't Seth's mum's.

Seth took a deep breath as he walked towards her door. He was thinking about Nadiya's idea to tackle the amphitheatre haunting. He wanted it to be a plan, but he knew it was madness, something

they'd never be able to do. Not really. He'd have to tell Nadiya that when he saw her.

Rafik was waiting for him, creating a sense of calm amid the chaos. The white walls and lights behind him shone bright.

"Seth? Before you go in, I need to tell you something."

Seth swallowed. Tell him what?

"Your mum," Rafik went on. "She doesn't look great in there. And she won't be able to speak to you. She probably won't wake up, not even for you. But that's normal. The treatment is going well. So please don't be worried."

"OK," Seth said. "Thanks." And he went in.

The room was dark, and too warm, with that faint tinge of disinfectant.

As Seth's eyes became accustomed to the light, he saw his mum. She was hooked up to even more

wires and tubes this time, liquid and electric pulses going into her, coming out of her.

Her face was blank like a mask.

Seth took her hand, his fingers feeling for the pulse beating in her wrist. Then he twined his fingers with hers and stared at her unmoving face. Her fingers didn't move either. Seth rested his face on her hand and closed his eyes.

He had never felt so lonely.

"Mum," he whispered. "Mum, don't go ..."

Then she sat up.

Seth gasped and recoiled, leaning away from her. He saw that her body was still flat on the bed. But, at the same time, she was sitting up, her face moving, eyes sparkling.

Seth knew at once that this was her shadow. It was her shadow that was sitting up. Not her body. Horror flooded him as he realised what this meant.

21

Seth's mum held her arms out to him. And he was tempted, so tempted, to hug her. But he knew he couldn't hug his mum's shadow. He had to hug her body.

So, ignoring the shadow's open arms, Seth kneeled down and hugged his mum, hugged her hard, eyes screwed tight, until he felt her body's warmth through her bedsheets and his clothes.

She was alive. Not a shadow.

She was his mum.

When Seth at last opened his eyes the shadow had gone. His mum was just his mum, lying on the hospital bed. Her breath shallow, but steady, moving in and out of her body as regular as the clock on the wall.

Seth staggered in disbelief. It was nine already. Three hours had gone by.

The door opened and Rafik came in. "She'll be conscious tomorrow," he said in his gentle voice. "You'll see."

"I'd better go," Seth said, confused. "My friend will be waiting."

"OK," Rafik said. "But, Seth, you did the right thing. Your mum will have known you were there, sleeping next to her. You helped keep her safe."

*

Seth took the lift. He was too tired to walk.

When the lift doors shut, Seth noticed his own reflection in the shiny metal doors. His face was pale and puffy with tears, but he couldn't remember crying.

What had happened in that room? Had he really seen Mum's shadow? Had he kept her safe, like Rafik said? Had he stopped her dying?

Seth shuddered and wiped his eyes. It didn't matter. His mum was alive. And Rafik had said she was going to get better, so she was going to get better. That's what Seth told himself. But, even so, he could feel that darkness threatening him. Like a flood of cold black water pressing on his chest, rising up to his nose and mouth.

The darkness rose and Seth felt like he would drown in it.

He stepped back and punched the lift door with

his hands. The lift shuddered to a halt and an alarm went off. And, in the few seconds before the lift started again, Seth made a decision.

He had to stop this. He had to push the darkness away again

And so they'd do it.

Tonight.

He and Nadiya would carry out her masterplan. Seth wanted the fear, he craved it. The risk. The danger. If he didn't feel the fear tonight, he'd have to face that cold tide of blackness again.

22

The helicopter came out of the sky like a spaceship.

Its searchlight rippled over the crowds of party guests, followed by the updraft from the machine's rotor blades, which filled the air with dust and sand from the amphitheatre.

Seth and Nadiya had walked a full circuit of the building site, identifying hundreds of security guards, dozens of TV crews and five police roadblocks. The weird thing was all the waiting staff were dressed as Roman centurions. There were Roman banners on display everywhere.

Twice Nadiya asked Seth how his mum was.

Twice Seth said she was fine. But he added no detail.

Since then Nadiya had stopped asking.

The guests were entering at the main gate. Everyone was dressed up – the men in dinner suits and the women in fancy dresses, clutching sparkly handbags. As they went in, each guest was given a white hard hat with their name on the peak and a Renaissance logo on the back.

"How on earth do *we* get in?" Seth asked.

Nadiya had been watching carefully. "There," she suggested.

"No way," Seth said. "The security's too tight."

"Let's wait until the next chopper comes in then," Nadiya said.

Almost immediately another helicopter flew in from behind a tower block. The security staff on the gate held down sheets of paper and hard hats, as the air swirled. Guests shielded their eyes. Waiters tried to stop their capes furling out. Dust from the excavations flurried in whirlwinds around them.

"Follow me," Nadiya said. "*Now*."

They weaved in among the crowds waiting to be let in. They kept low so as not to be seen by the security guards and CCTV. At last they reached the entrance. Paused. Listened. Another helicopter came in.

"*Now*," Nadiya said.

23

Nadiya and Seth scrambled under the table where staff were distributing badges and hard hats. As the wind picked up and clusters of guests covered their hair with scarves, held onto their long dresses, Nadiya reached onto the table and grabbed two hard hats.

She crawled to the end of the table so they were by the doors to the building site.

Seth followed. Past the line of shiny shoes

visible from under the tablecloth. Past the cries of people trying to protect their eyes from the dust.

Then, out into the fenced-off amphitheatre. Nadiya and Seth tracked a couple who looked about the right age to be their parents, hoping people would think they were together.

They went down a red carpet and into the great marquee. Last night it had been full of zombie slaves, but it was now stuffed with party guests and the sour smell of alcohol.

A huge white canopy held up by ropes on the outside and inside. Bright strobing colours that shimmered on the walls and ceiling. Tables and chairs adorned with Roman-style wreaths. And waiters in long white robes, tied by golden cords.

"This is like a bad amusement park," Nadiya complained. Seth nodded. She was spot on. It looked cheap and glitzy.

"Where are the slaves?" Nadiya said, her voice low.

Seth grabbed two orange juices and handed one to Nadiya. He'd been so pumped with adrenalin that he'd not sensed the slaves. Or seen them. Yet.

He studied all the ways in and out of the marquee. The waiters. The security guards. The men in suits. And then he saw a fenced-off break in the floor, where the wooden planks didn't reach.

There was movement there now.

Seth looked hard into the crumbling shadows and saw eyes peering up into the light. Men in rags, carrying weapons. Men with fury etched onto their faces. Seth sensed trouble brewing. The slaves had seen the Roman symbols and the centurions and the togas. They were bound to strike.

"Steady," Nadiya said, reading Seth's mind. "We can sort this."

"It won't be easy," he countered.

"But we can." Nadiya's words hit Seth like iron. "No way am I letting Renaissance get away with their modern-day slavery."

24

"Ladies and gentlemen …"

From the edge of the amphitheatre, a woman's voice boomed out of a circle of speakers at the crowd gathered on the red carpets. The voice was soft and calm, the accent Italian.

Two hundred people turned to face the tall, dark-haired woman standing on a raised platform. The noise of their chatter faded.

The woman paused, then smiled.

"Good evening, London. I am Francesca Caesari, President of Renaissance Holdings. Renaissance are intensely proud to build the UK's most state-of-the-art sports stadium. And the fact that this is happening alongside the UK's oldest stadium – this magnificent amphitheatre – feels very special, very magical."

Her words were met by a roar of approval and applause.

Nadiya glanced at Seth. Her face looked like it had when she'd eaten that slice of lemon in the museum café.

"At Renaissance, we feel we are the new Romans. Romans of the twenty-first century. We are building stadiums across Europe and beyond." Caesari paused. "But in our stadiums we will not be killing animals for our amusement."

Seth was taken aback by the audience's loud laughter at this 'joke'.

"And nor," Caesari went on, laughing too, enjoying her moment, "will we be forcing hundreds of British slaves to do the work for us."

More laughter and a few whistles. Francesca Caesari had the audience in the palm of her hand.

Seth glanced at Nadiya. His friend looked furious. She'd need that anger to push her through the next hour if they were to carry out their plan.

"This time –" Caesari raised her voice – "we will pay the British to build the stadium for us. And we won't beat them to death if they slack for a moment or take a lunch break ..."

Nadiya's face was flushed and fierce. Her eyes fixed in a death stare on Caesari.

Then, as the wave of smug laughter died down, a shout. "What about the slaves in Sri Lanka, Caesari? Your sweatshops where employees are sacked for –?"

Seth and Nadiya span round to see a young woman wrapped in a flag with a golden lion on a dark red background. Then they saw four security guards move in fast and drag her down, a beefy hand clamped over her mouth. In seconds she was gone.

Seth felt Nadiya's hand grip his arm. He looked into his friend's eyes and saw rage burning there.

"Now," she said. "The plan. We need to do it now. Caesari can't get away with it. Are you in?"

Seth didn't hesitate.

"I'm in," he said.

25

As Caesari's speech drew to an end, Nadiya pulled at Seth. "Come on," she urged. "She's already heading upstairs."

Seth followed his friend as she edged through the guests to the door at the foot of the stone steps.

It was time to carry out their plan. Time to unleash the dead.

Seth went to the door where he could hear the ghost slaves shouting and banging.

"I can't open it."

"It's bolted," Nadiya said, cursing. "How do we get in?"

It was a good question. How on earth would two kids get into a locked part of a high-security amphitheatre? And then unleash a ghostly mass of angry slaves?

"What about this?" Nadiya said, pointing to an iron rod stuck in the ground. On top of it was a flag with the Roman symbol of an eagle on. "Let's use this."

"How?" Seth said.

"The iron rod can lever the door open –"

"Then we can wave the flag to get the slaves to follow me," Seth said, catching on.

But he could hardly believe what he was saying. Could he really do this? Could their plan really work?

"*Come on*," Nadiya urged. "We need to move fast."

They pulled the iron rod out of the ground and wedged it behind the bolt on the door. Then they used all their strength to pull it away.

It didn't budge.

"Further up," Nadiya said. "We'll get more leverage if we pull from higher up."

They tried again, and again. At first, nothing. Then a crack, and the clasp and lock tore from the wall.

No one else reacted. They were transfixed on Francesca Caesari, still clapping as she disappeared up the stairs.

Seth opened the door slowly and peered into the darkness.

Dozens and then hundreds of eyes stared back at him.

The slaves.

It was time.

Seth swung the eagle flag above his head and roared like a warrior leading his troops into battle. He could feel all the tension pouring out of him.

He smiled inside at how good it felt to roar like that.

And the slaves came. Their faces creased with rage as they saw the eagle banner in Seth's hands. And this time they moved faster, much faster.

Seth scrambled up the steps, the banner aloft, desperate to get out of the slaves' way.

Why are they not slow, like last time? he thought in panic. *They're moving too fast for the plan to work.*

Seth steadied himself. All of a sudden, the danger was intense, real, life-threatening.

26

Seth sprinted through the crowd, his Roman banner billowing above him. The guests parted, seeming to think Seth and Nadiya were part of the whole Renaissance performance.

But then they turned to see the ghostly army of slaves funnelling out of the bowl of the amphitheatre towards them – and someone shouted, "ZOMBIES!"

Instant panic.

The very idea of zombies in their midst caused total havoc. Guests ran every which way, screaming in terror.

But the outraged howls of the dead drowned out the screams of the living.

As he ran, Seth saw Nadiya sprint past him and push on up the staircase.

"This way," she gasped. "It's working. They're coming."

Seth went up after her, three steps at a time, his legs on fire. The metal frame of the staircase shook at first. But when it stopped shaking Seth knew why. The slaves were on the steps too, weighing them down.

As Seth and Nadiya reached the top, three security guards stood barring their way, arms crossed over their chests. But when they saw a flood of zombies moving towards them their faces went pale and their mouths gaped open.

They fled.

With the guards gone, Nadiya grabbed Seth's banner and yanked it through the doorway, Seth attached to the other end. She turned right. Seth – and the slaves – followed her.

Down a corridor and round another corner they ran. At the sound of Caesari's voice they pushed on.

Then they came to a double door of glowing wood, with gold handles. And, in front of it, more guards in dark suits.

Four of them.

Legs apart, arms locked in front of them, all four were pointing guns down the corridor at Seth and Nadiya.

The biggest guard steadied himself.

"*Arresto!*" he shouted in Italian. "Stop! Or we fire."

"Then fire!" Seth yelled as he walked towards the guards, Nadiya at his side.

27

Seth could see the guards' eyes now. He tried to work out what they were thinking, what they might do. At first, he saw confusion. They might be trained in the use of firearms, but they didn't want to shoot at unarmed children, not even to protect Caesari and Renaissance.

Second, he saw horror, as the corridor thronged with a ragged mass of men whose stink clogged the air, making it impossible to breathe.

Bewildered, the guards froze. Seth walked past them and pushed open the door.

And there, in a semi-circle of leather chairs, was the board of directors of Renaissance. At the centre was Francesca Caesari, her face flushed nearly as bright as her suit from the buzz of her speech.

"What the ..." she gasped. "Guards!"

Seth looked past her into a small room behind the board room. A boy and a girl were on the floor, playing with a box of wooden blocks. They had the same dark-haired look as Caesari. No doubt about it – they were her children.

Caesari was standing now, fists on the polished table in front of her, expecting to see her security guards appear. Instead, she was confronted with the monstrous horde behind Seth.

Shouts. Screams. Gunshots. The ear-splitting *crack* of gunfire.

The four guards fired again and again at the army of slaves, now that Seth and Nadiya were out of the way.

The two little children put down their blocks and began to sob and wail.

Seth could see that the bullets were having no effect. You can't gun down the dead. And the dead were intent on the board room.

Francesca Caesari was standing right in front of her children now, her hands white-knuckled as she pressed down on the table. She opened her mouth, but no words formed. Her children were big-eyed and silent too.

Seth could see that all the adults were paralysed by fear, confusion and panic.

"We can stop this." Nadiya broke the silence.

"What *is* this?" Caesari demanded. "My children ..."

"We can stop this," Nadiya repeated. "No one will get hurt. They have come for a purpose."

"Then stop them," Caesari yelled, her eyes flitting from Nadiya to the slaves, to her children.

"Seth?" Nadiya ordered. "Stop them."

Seth turned to face the slaves.

His legs trembled in terror. But he needed to do this. He had no idea if it would work. But he had to try.

28

Seth raised his hands, both palms facing the ragged army of slaves.

The slaves fell silent and kneeled.

There was a gasp.

Seth gasped too. He couldn't believe what he had done. He looked at the slaves and they lifted their eyes from the ground. He heard them mutter *Angylesau* again.

Angel. He was an angel to them. An angel like

he'd been to the Anglo-Saxon villagers in Halifax.

"Whoever you are," Caesari said. "Send these zombies away. Please."

"They are *not* zombies," Nadiya seethed.

"Whoever they are, send them away," Caesari implored.

"No," Nadiya said. "Not until you listen to them."

"No?" Caesari's voice was no longer confident. She wasn't used to being contradicted.

"Not until you listen," Nadiya said.

"OK." Caesari's eyes flicked to her children again. Seth could see that they were more important to her than anything right now.

"These people are slaves," Nadiya began. "Not zombies. They are the ghosts of the slaves who built this amphitheatre. The ones you joked about in your speech. And the reason you can see them is that they are angry."

"You expect me to believe they are ghosts?" Caesari scoffed, her tone arrogant once more.

"Your security guards just fired shot after shot at them. None of the slaves went down. Did they?"

Caesari closed her eyes and nodded. She pressed the tips of her fingers together. "So what has this got to do with me?"

Nadiya narrowed her eyes. "Are you for real?" she said, under her breath. Then, "They are angry with you," in a loud, clear voice.

"Me?" Caesari replied, shocked.

"You want to know why they're angry with you?" Nadiya asked.

Caesari nodded. Her skin was pale, her eyes red and her hands trembled on the table.

"Because your company uses slaves to make cheap sportswear in Sri Lanka – and all around the world. And these slaves of the past won't go away or let this stadium be built until you commit to looking after your workers properly."

"This is preposterous," one of the board directors said, slapping his hands down hard. He moved towards Nadiya, grabbing her arm.

In a sudden, animal movement, one of the slaves jumped up and pulled the man onto the floor. Then, standing over him, he placed an axe against his throat.

The man whimpered.

And Seth – like everyone else in the room – held his breath. One of Caesari's children began to wail again.

What would Francesca Caesari say?

And, even if she promised to improve the lives of her workers, would her promises put a stop to the slaves' deadly anger?

29

Francesca Caesari gazed at her children, then back around the table at her directors. None of them dared to look up from the papers in front of them. Nor to look at the man who was lying on the floor, an axe to his throat.

Now what?

Caesari stood. She looked like the boss of Renaissance again – her face was resolute, her eyes glinted with their sharp edge.

"I can't just change everything," she argued. "We employ tens of thousands of people. And these men, these slaves? They would have been given food and a bed by the Romans. In those days that was more than most people had."

Seth turned his gaze to Nadiya. He knew she'd have an answer for that.

"In Sri Lanka – in your sweatshops – there are children the same age as yours. Working and dying. That awful factory fire last year. That was your fault."

"Is it up to me to check every factory in the world?" Caesari snapped. She was bold now. Defensive.

Seth saw that the slave ghosts were restless. They had begun to move aside, making a channel up their centre. He stared into the gap to see that slaves from the back were coming forward.

As they came closer, Seth could see that they weren't adults.

"*Mio dio!*" Caesari sobbed. "God in heaven."

A mass of children emerged and sat calmly in the gap between the adult slaves and the board room.

They were thin and pale, their clothes in tatters. Some had raw wounds on their feet and arms. Each one stared at Francesca Caesari, unblinking.

Seth saw tiny beams of light pass from each child to Caesari. Narrow golden threads attached them to her.

Caesari looked at the ghost children, one by one. Then at her own children who were standing behind her, alarmed and distressed.

Nobody spoke.

Not a murmur.

The moment of silence stretched out until Caesari reached to touch the threads of light coming towards her, as if they were irritating her like the silk of spiders' webs.

"What?" Caesari pleaded. "What can I do?"

Nadiya glanced at Seth. For the first time she looked unsure of what she should say.

"These children." Seth took over, the words coming to him as if from afar. "You can see the threads of light, can't you?"

Caesari nodded, solemn.

"They are yours now."

"Mine?" Caesari said. "What do you mean?"

"The children are attached to you," Seth told her. "They will be with you."

"With me?"

"They are yours to protect and keep safe – until you change your ways."

Caesari shook her head, stepped back. Her two children grabbed for her.

"But what can I do?" she asked, as if helpless.

And Seth remembered the words his mum had passed on to him. The message from his dad. Seth knew that when confronted with the shadows of the past, he had to do the right thing.

"You must do what you think is right," Seth told Caesari, repeating his dad's words.

30

When Seth arrived at Ward 5 the next morning, Rafik smiled at him and gave him the thumbs-up. Seth took it as a good sign.

And it was.

Mum was sitting up in her bed, when he walked in. "Hey, love," she said, her voice a bit croaky.

She was watching the TV news. Seth saw the face of Francesca Caesari staring back at him from the screen.

"Pass me the remote," Mum said. "I'll turn it off."

Seth walked around the bed. He felt his mum's eyes following him. Then he leaned down to hug her.

Seth took the remote and flicked the TV off. But not before he heard Caesari announce that she was changing the way her company worked. No more sweatshops, she promised. Investment in communities in Sri Lanka, she said.

Mum smiled as Seth sat back down. Seth worried that she looked as pale and thin as the day before when she'd been out cold. But he said nothing.

Then he waited.

Mum breathed out deeply. "The doctor said …" She hesitated. "The doctor said … the treatment has been a success. So far. We have to wait a few more days now."

Seth wanted to speak, but he knew that any words would come out as a huge sob. So he just nodded and smiled.

Seth and his mum stared into each other's eyes.

Another silence. Seth could see his mum was as full of emotion as he was.

His phone pinged. He had no doubt it was a message from Nadiya asking if he'd seen the news. She was at her aunt's, following it on TV.

"The doctor says you and I should make a list," Mum said at last.

"A list of what?" Seth asked.

"A list of things we really want to do or see. To inspire us to do them."

"Right." Seth didn't know how to react.

"It's part of the treatment plan," Mum said more clearly now. "To make us better."

"Go on then," Seth said, showing her the notebook he'd bought at the Museum of London. "I'll write the list. You tell me what you want to do."

"It's for both of us, Seth. It's a list for both of us. It's for you as much as it is for me."

Seth understood. "I know. But you go first," he said.

Mum eased back onto the bed.

"I need to sit on a beach in Cornwall with you." She sighed. "Listen to the waves, dip my feet in the sea."

Seth nodded and wrote it down.

"Now you," Mum said.

"I want to watch England play at Wembley."

Seth saw his mum smile, as he wrote his wish down.

"Before the end of the year?" he added.

"Deal," Mum said.

Seth laughed and they carried on, making a list of things to look forward to.

"One more," Mum said weakly, as if tired all of a sudden. "Your turn."

Seth delved into his mind. He thought about what he and Nadiya had endured at the site of the Morti Stadium over the last few days. How once again they had defended the people of the past and of the present, kept them from suffering. Deep down, Seth wished all that would end – so he could look after his mum. So life could be normal again.

But Seth wanted his mum's wishes to come true. More than anything, that's what he wanted.

"I'd like to go home." Seth grinned. "Then to a Cornish beach when you're well enough."

Seth didn't know if they would ever make it to that beach, but his mum smiled and closed her eyes, as if she could feel the sea breeze already.

Seth squeezed her hand, not imagining for a minute that Cornwall was where he'd need his powers as a Defender more than ever.

ARE YOU A HISTORY BUFF OR A HISTORY BUFFOON?

Take this *difficilis** QUIZ to find out how much YOU know about the Romans and the Britons!

1. What stopped the Romans' first attempt to invade Britain?

A. The people of Britain fought the Romans on the beaches and drove them back to their ships.

B. The weather was so bad that the Romans gave up till the sun came out.

C. The Romans forgot their passports and had to go home to get them.

* That's Latin for 'difficult'.

2. How do we know about the Romans' time in Britain?

A. From paintings on the walls of old Roman buildings.

B. From books written by the Britons of the time.

C. From letters, books and other documents written by Roman writers of the time.

3. Where were most of the soldiers in the Roman army that came to Britain from?

A. Africa, France, Germany, the Balkans, Spain and the Middle East.

B. Italy – only Roman citizens could be in the Roman army.

C. Everywhere – anyone could join the Roman army as long as he had his own sword and shield.

4. Which city was the capital of Roman Britain?

A. Eboracum – York.

B. Londinium – London.

C. Camulodunum – Colchester.

5. Which animals did the Romans bring on their ships to help with their invasion of Britain?

A. Elephants.

B. Wolves.

C. Ostriches.

6. Who did most of the hard work in Roman Britain?

A. Roman centurions.

B. Slaves.

C. Specialist contractors from Italy.

7. What were Roman amphitheatres used for?

A. Staged fights between men and animals.

B. Huge football matches – called *calcio* in Latin.

C. Performances of a special kind of Roman musical theatre.

8. What were the native women in Roman Britain allowed to do that the Roman women weren't?

A. Referee the football matches in the amphitheatres.

B. Work as clerks in the tax office in the capital city.

C. Train as warriors and rule as queens.

9. Which ruler in Britain paid the Romans taxes, instead of going to war against them?

A. Cartimandua.

B. Henry VIII.

C. Boudicca.

10. Why did the Romans leave Britain about 400 years after Julius Caesar first arrived in 55 BC?

A. It was too cold and wet and they had vitamin D deficiency because the sun never shone.

B. Warriors from Scotland, Ireland and Germany kept attacking and the Romans were losing control.

C. London's city wall and Hadrian's Wall both fell down at the same time.

Answers on the next page ☛

ANSWERS

1. B
Wild weather and a fierce storm in the English Channel were too much for the Romans. They gave up and decided to come back on a calm, sunny day.

2. C
Everything we know about the Romans' time in Britain was written by the Romans, and by a Greek author called Cassius Dio too. The people of Britain were illiterate. This means the history we know is told from a Roman point of view – it doesn't include what the people of Britain thought or experienced.

3. A&B
The 'Legionaries' in the Roman army had to be Roman citizens. They were the elite of the army. But the rest of the army were 'Auxiliaries' – soldiers recruited from the countries the Roman army invaded. These recruits didn't have much choice, but if they survived 25 years in the army their reward was Roman citizenship!

4. C
Colchester was the original capital of Roman Britain. London became the capital after the revolt led by Boudicca.

5. A

Nobody in Britain had ever seen elephants before. These huge animals filled people with fear and wonder. And that is exactly why the Romans brought them!

6. B

The Roman Empire was built upon the use of slaves – people captured and forced to work for no money. The local Britons kept slaves too, and so did the Anglo-Saxons who came after them, and the Vikings too.

7. A

The Romans brought exotic animals – and armed men called gladiators – to the amphitheatres to fight one another to the death. These displays were hugely popular and hugely violent. The Colosseum at Rome seated 50,000 people and 1,000s of men and animals fought and died there.

8. C

The women of Britain at this time could be warriors and rulers. The Romans did not like women to do these jobs. In particular, they disapproved of the women who were queens.

133

9. A

Cartimandua was Queen of the Brigantes, a Celtic people of the 1st century AD. She made a pact with the Romans to keep her people safe. Boudicca, Queen of the Iceni, refused to make a pact. She led an uprising against the Romans and many of her people died.

10. B

The whole of the Roman Empire was under attack. The Romans left Britain so they could keep control of a smaller empire. This left Britain open to invasion by peoples from Germany and elsewhere.

BUFF OR BUFFOON?

If you scored 10/10

You're a top-class history buff. Seth and Nadiya will be glad to have you on their side as Defenders!

If you scored 5-9

You have more research to do before the Defenders will add you to their team!

If you scored 4 or under

Seth and Nadiya won't mind. They are history whizz-kids and will gladly give you a lesson!

Acknowledgements

Thanks, first, to my wife and daughter who read my drafts and give me very direct feedback, and who support me in a million other ways. They are my world – and without them there would be no books.

Thanks are due to Emma Hargrave, for her excellent and sensitive editorial guidance on *Dark Arena*. Thanks, too, to all at Barrington Stoke, who help me live the dream of being a published author!

I am grateful to the children and teachers at Newcastle School for Boys, whose ideas have helped me so much with the Defenders books.

Thanks to the Museum of London and the Guildhall Museum, where I did some of my research. And particular thanks to my neighbours for lending Seth their dog, Rosa, and to the real Seth White, for the use of his brilliant name.

About Tom Palmer

Tom Palmer is the author of forty books for children. His books feature sport, spies, detectives, ghosts and history – and sometimes a combination of all these things!

In 2016 Tom went to Rome and saw the famous Colosseum. This awe-inspiring place gave Tom the idea for *Dark Arena*. That and the fact that there is an amphitheatre still buried beneath London's streets today. You can visit a part of it in the Guildhall Museum. The museum is near the London Museum, which is a fantastic introduction to what life in the city has been like through the ages. (The café serves great cakes too!)

Tom lives in Halifax in Yorkshire – just like Seth does – with his family and a cat called Katniss. He used to have a cat called Gus, but Gus died while Tom was writing *Dark Arena*. And so, Tom gave Gus a cameo role in this book – he's the cat at Nadiya's aunt's house.

Tom visits schools up and down the country to talk about his books. Find out more at www.tompalmer.co.uk.